Dedicated with love
to my mother

Art created with watercolor wash and graphite and colored pencil
on hot pressed watercolor paper
Typeset in Filosofia
Hand lettering by Vincent X. Kirsch and David Gatti
Book design by Vincent X. Kirsch and Donna Mark

Published by Bloomsbury U.S.A. Children's Books
175 Fifth Avenue, New York, New York 10010
Distributed to the trade by Macmillan

Library of Congress Cataloging-in-Publication Data
Kirsch, Vincent X.
Natalie & Naughtily / Vincent X. Kirsch. — 1st U.S. ed.
p.   cm.
Summary: Natalie and Naughtily Nopps live above their family's
department store and love to play there, but one particularly busy day
they discover that "helping" is even better than playing.
ISBN-13: 978-1-59990-269-2 · ISBN-10: 1-59990-269-9 (hardcover)
ISBN-13: 978-1-59990-320-0 · ISBN-10: 1-59990-320-2 (reinforced)
[1. Department stores—Fiction. 2. Sisters—Fiction. 3. Humorous stories.]
I. Title. II. Title: Natalie and Naughtily.
PZ7.K6383Nat 2008   [E]—dc22   2007051098

First U.S. Edition 2008
Printed in China
2 4 6 8 10 9 7 5 3 1 (hardcover)
2 4 6 8 10 9 7 5 3 1 (reinforced)

© **Mixed Sources**
Product group from well-managed
forests, controlled sources and
recycled wood or fibre
FSC www.fsc.org Cert no. SCS-COC-00927
© 1996 Forest Stewardship Council

NATALIE & NAUGHTILY

VINCENT X. KIRSCH

BLOOMSBURY
CHILDREN'S
BOOKS

Natalie and Naughtily Nopps lived in a house on top of the greatest department store in the world. Did you notice that it is a department store with their name on it? *Well, did you?*

From the time they were born, Natalie did things one way
and Naughtily did them another.

When they were big enough to visit the store, Natalie wanted to go
that way and Naughtily wanted to go this way.

At bedtime, Natalie knew just what kind of story she wanted to hear: "There must be at least one happy ending and two cash registers." But it was never what Naughtily wanted to hear: "There must be two happy endings and one escalator!"

When asked what they wanted for their birthdays, Natalie said:
"To play on every floor of the store from top to bottom!" And Naughtily?
"From bottom to top!"

Rainy days were the only time the girls were allowed to play in the store—
and they loved those days best of all. When the weather was sunny, the two
girls had exactly the same thing to say: "If only it would rain!"

One rainy day, Stillman, the butler, handed them a note from their parents.

Dear Natalie and Naughtily:

*Today is going to be a very, very busy day. It would be a great help
if you did not play in the store.*

"Today we will not play in the store," they both said. "Today we shall go to
the store to help!"

The first floor of Nopps Department Store was busy indeed. Stepforth, the elevator operator, said, "A busy store is no place for little girls to play." But Natalie and Naughtily were there to help.

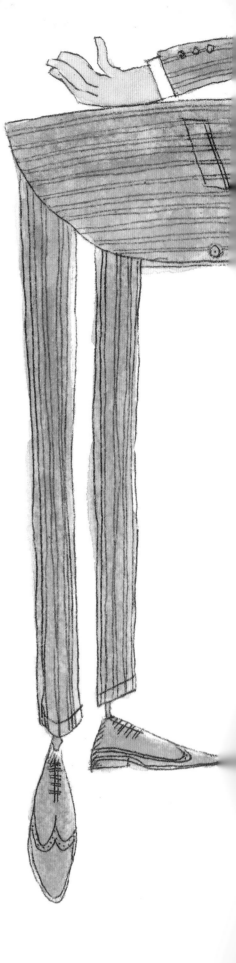

Natalie announced, "Welcome to Nopps, the greatest department store in the world. I'm here to help."

A customer appeared. "My name is Rudy Toolittle. I would like to see every floor in the store."

"No one knows every floor better than I," said Natalie, "but I am very busy right now." So Natalie gave Rudy a list of her favorite things on every floor.

At the same time, another customer tapped Naughtily on the elbow. "Pardon me, madam," he said. "I am Ridley Toolittle. Would you please show me the way to the top floor?"

"That is my favorite thing to do," Naughtily said, "but I am helping today." Naughtily handed her very own map to Ridley and sent him on his way.

Mr. Iceberger, the store manager, told the two Nopps girls, "It would be a great help if you went back upstairs." Natalie and Naughtily hurried up—but only as far as the second floor.

On the second floor, the customers were making a great fuss over the latest evening gowns by the world-famous designer Dandileoni. Natalie and Naughtily knew just how to help. Natalie helped six of the fussiest customers.

Naughtily helped six even fussier ones.

"My beautiful dresses were not made for little girls to play with!" said Dandileoni furiously. So Natalie and Naughtily scurried up to the third floor.

On the third floor, the new spring hats and a perfume called Mischief #5 had just arrived. Natalie and Naughtily knew just how to help. Natalie picked out a spring hat for everyone.

Naughtily wanted everyone to sample Mischief #5.

"This floor is no place for little girls to play," said a customer who had been drenched in Mischief #5. So Natalie and Naughtily sped up to the fourth floor.

On the fourth floor there was a big sale on winter coats that
no one wanted to buy. Natalie and Naughtily knew just how to help.
Natalie sold two coats for the price of one.

Naughtily sold one coat for the price of two.

"*Pssst!* This floor is no place for little girls to play," whispered the store detective, Mr. Spygoggle. So Natalie and Naughtily sneaked up to the fifth floor.

There were not enough salespeople on the fifth floor to show off the latest gizmos and gadgets sold exclusively at Nopps. Natalie and Naughtily knew just how to help. Natalie showed off the new-and-improved automatic-flying-rainbow-making umbrella.

Naughtily showed off the do-it-yourself twelve-legged cat-catcher gadget.

"This floor is no place for little girls to play," a pocket-size know-botty robot remarked. So Natalie and Naughtily wandered off to the sixth floor.

ASK FOR HELP
DO NOT EVER TOUCH ANYTHING

On the sixth floor, a very important customer was looking for something incredibly rare and very old. Natalie and Naughtily knew just how to help. Natalie found a unicorn that was incredibly rare. Naughtily discovered a dinosaur that was very old.

NO
CHILDREN
NO
PLAYING
NO
TOUCHING

6

"The next floor would be a perfect place for little girls to play,"
said Mrs. Finegloss, an incredibly snooty and very old salesperson.
When Natalie and Naughtily remembered what was on the seventh
floor, they raced up as quickly as they could.

The seventh floor was the toy floor. No one would mind if they were on this floor. Both girls wanted to help, but Natalie could not get away from the customers chasing after the last Daisy Duzwell doll.

Naughtily could not control the mob
fighting to be next for the "Race to Mars"
ride.

"This floor is no place for little girls to
help," Natalie and Naughtily admitted to a
big purple squirrel as they escaped to the
eighth floor.

The store tailor, Ago Forbici, had a crowd of customers waiting for alterations on the eighth floor. Natalie and Naughtily knew just how to help. Natalie measured her customers one at a time.

Naughtily measured her customers all at once.

"Zizziz nottle a plotz furzi nittle gurzles!" Ago Forbici told his assistant, who translated it for her assistant, who translated it for his assistant, who told Natalie and Naughtily that this was no place for little girls to play. So Natalie and Naughtily left for the ninth floor.

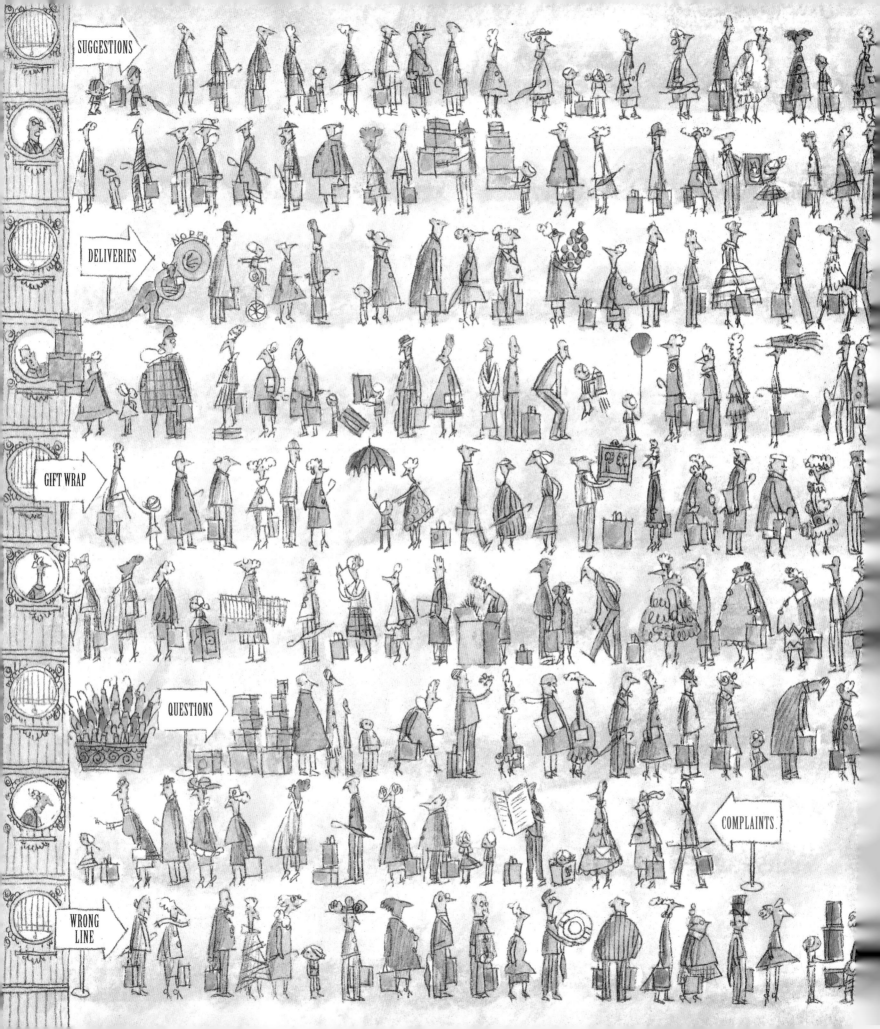

SUGGESTIONS

DELIVERIES

GIFT WRAP

QUESTIONS

COMPLAINTS

WRONG
LINE

DIRECTIONS

REPAIRS

LOST

FOUND

On the ninth floor, there were lines everywhere. One was
full of the customers Natalie had helped. Another was full of the
customers Naughtily had helped. Mr. Iceberger told the two Nopps
girls, "It would be a great help if you went all the way upstairs. A busy
store is no place for little girls who have not been any help all day."

Suddenly two happy customers appeared.

"I have seen every floor of the store!" said Rudy Toolittle. "What a brilliant list!"

"And I made it all the way to the top!" said Ridley Toolittle. "What a marvelous map!"

"Nopps is the greatest department store in the world!" Ridley and Rudy said at the same time.

Natalie knew that Rudy Toolittle had not really seen every floor.
Naughtily knew that Ridley Toolittle had not really reached the top.
Natalie and Naughtily knew just how to help.

Natalie and Naughtily Nopps took the two little Toolittles all the way upstairs and gave them a private tour of their house on top of the greatest department store in the world.

"And did you notice," Natalie and Naughtily asked at the same time, "that it is a department store with our name on it?"

Well, did you?

My favorites

first floor
A balloon-inflating machine
A statue of the squirrel king
Six goldfish

Second floor
A giant lady's shoe
Naughtily's kite
My Daisy Duzwell doll

third floor
A perfume with my name on it
A parrot that makes announcements
The butterfly-catching hat

fourth floor
A box of ~~extra~~ my buttons
Christmas decorations
A snow-making machine

fifth floor
A salesman with socks of different colors
Escalator on and off buttons
A spider and a spider web

sixth floor
A mummy with a feather duster
Mrs. Finegloss's vacuum cleaner
A ghost

seventh floor
An alien spy camera
A three-wheeled bicycle
Santa Claus's chair

Eighth floor
A cat named Thimble
A magical top hat
The flag from Ago Forbici's country

Ninth floor
A collection of lost umbrellas
The kangaroo that plays a tuba
Naughtily's toy giraffe

♡ by Natalie Nopps

Naughtily Nopps's Map of Nopps Department Store!!!

Me!!